Swing High, Swing Low

A Book of Opposites

written by Fiona Coward
illustrated by Giovanni Manna

Barefoot Books
Celebrating Art and Story

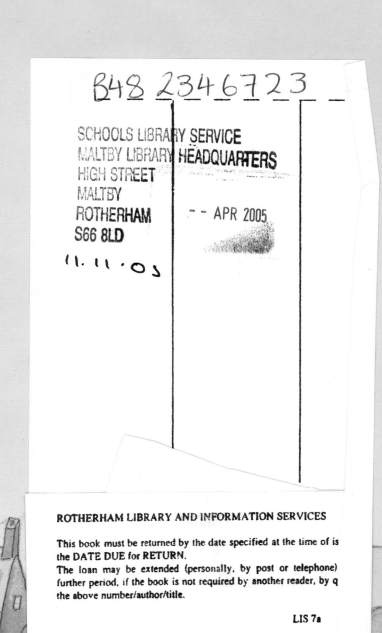

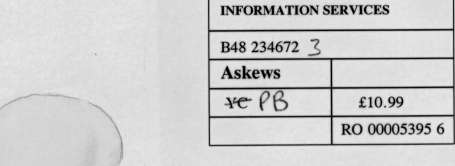

Up the ladder,
down the stairs.

Under the table,
over the chairs.

Tummy says 'yes',
    Mummy says 'no'.

Red says stop.
Green says go.

White is light,
black is dark.

Run to the gate,
walk through the park.

Puddles are wet,
feet are dry.

Swing low to the ground,
then high in the sky.

A time to work
and a time to play.

Mess it all up,
then tidy away.

Joe makes me laugh,
Kate makes me cry.

Call 'hello'
and wave 'goodbye'.

The sun is hot,
    ice cream is cold.

Babies are young,
grandparents old.

Whisper a secret,
try not to shout.

Bring in the washing,
put the cat out.

Pull up the covers,
    roll down the sheet.

The moon is awake,
but the house is asleep.

For my daughters, Erin and Megan — F. C.
A Miriam, per i suoi preziosi consigli — G. M.

Barefoot Books
124 Walcot Street
Bath BA1 5BG

This book was typeset in Infant Calligraphic Bold 30pt
The illustrations were prepared in china ink and watercolour on watercolour paper

Graphic design by Nicky Jex, Henley-on-Thames
Colour separation by Bright Arts Singapore
Printed and bound in Hong Kong by South China Printing

This book has been printed on 100% acid-free paper

Hardback ISBN 1-84148-162-9

British Cataloguing-in-Publication Data: a catalogue record for this book is
available from the British Library

1 3 5 7 9 8 6 4 2

Barefoot Books
Celebrating Art and Story

At Barefoot Books, we celebrate art and story with books that open the hearts and minds of children from all walks of life, inspiring them to read deeper, search further, and explore their own creative gifts. Taking our inspiration from many different cultures, we focus on themes that encourage independence of spirit, enthusiasm for learning, and acceptance of other traditions. Thoughtfully prepared by writers, artists and storytellers from all over the world, our products combine the best of the present with the best of the past to educate our children as the caretakers of tomorrow.

www.barefootbooks.com